Dear Parents:

Congratulations! Your child is taking the first steps on an exciting journey. The destination? Independent reading!

STEP INTO READING® will help your child get there. The program offers five steps to reading success. Each step includes fun stories and colorful art or photographs. In addition to original fiction and books with favorite characters, there are Step into Reading Non-Fiction Readers, Phonics Readers and Boxed Sets, Sticker Readers, and Comic Readers—a complete literacy program with something to interest every child.

Learning to Read, Step by Step!

Ready to Read   Preschool–Kindergarten
• big type and easy words • rhyme and rhythm • picture clues
For children who know the alphabet and are eager to begin reading.

Reading with Help   Preschool–Grade 1
• basic vocabulary • short sentences • simple stories
For children who recognize familiar words and sound out new words with help.

Reading on Your Own   Grades 1–3
• engaging characters • easy-to-follow plots • popular topics
For children who are ready to read on their own.

Reading Paragraphs   Grades 2–3
• challenging vocabulary • short paragraphs • exciting stories
For newly independent readers who read simple sentences with confidence.

Ready for Chapters   Grades 2–4
• chapters • longer paragraphs • full-color art
For children who want to take the plunge into chapter books but still like colorful pictures.

STEP INTO READING® is designed to give every child a successful reading experience. The grade levels are only guides; children will progress through the steps at their own speed, developing confidence in their reading. The F&P Text Level on the back cover serves as another tool to help you choose the right book for your child.

Remember, a lifetime love of reading starts with a single step!

All rights reserved. Published in the United States by Random House Children's Books, a division of Random House LLC, a Penguin Random House Company, New York. This work is adapted from *Everything Happens to Aaron in the Summer* by P. D. Eastman, copyright © 1967 and renewed 1995 by Random House LLC. The artwork herein originally appeared in *Everything Happens to Aaron in the Summer* and *The Cat in the Hat Beginner Book Dictionary. The Cat in the Hat Beginner Book Dictionary* by the Cat himself and P. D. Eastman, copyright © 1964 and renewed 1992 by Random House LLC.

Step into Reading, Random House, and the Random House colophon are registered trademarks of Random House LLC.

Visit us on the Web!
StepIntoReading.com
randomhousekids.com

Educators and librarians, for a variety of teaching tools, visit us at RHTeachersLibrarians.com

Library of Congress Cataloging-in-Publication Data
Eastman, P. D. (Philip D.)
Aaron has a lazy day / P. D. Eastman.
pages cm. — (Step into reading. Step 1 reader)
Summary: "Chronicles Aaron's attempts to beat the heat." —Provided by publisher.
ISBN 978-0-553-50844-4 (trade) — ISBN 978-0-375-97411-3 (lib. bdg.) —
ISBN 978-0-553-50845-1 (ebook)
[1. Ability—Fiction. 2. Alligators—Fiction. 3. Humorous stories.] I. Title.
PZ7.E1314Aar 2015 [E]—dc23 2014012165

Printed in the United States of America

10 9 8 7 6 5 4 3 2

This book has been officially leveled by using the F&P Text Level Gradient™ Leveling System.

Aaron
Has a
Lazy Day

by P. D. Eastman

Random House 🏠 New York

This is Aaron.

Aaron is an alligator.

Pleasant Hill Library
Contra Costa County Library
Monticello Ave.
Pleasant Hill, Ca. 94523
(925) 646-6434

Customer ID: **********5004

Items that you checked out

Title: Aaron has a lazy day /
:   31901060900281
Due: **Saturday, March 9, 2024**
Messages:
Item checked out.

Title: Math time at the apple orchard /
:   31901069371542
Due: **Saturday, March 9, 2024**
Messages:
Item checked out.

Title: Minnie's summer vacation /
:   31901069908046
Due: **Saturday, March 9, 2024**
Messages:
Item checked out.

Title: Perfect princess pets! : a collection of six
    early readers /
):   31901069548180
Due: **Saturday, March 9, 2024**
Messages:
Item checked out.

Title: Thanks for nothing! : a Little Bruce book /
):   31901066987431
Due: **Saturday, March 9, 2024**
Messages:
Item checked out.

Title: You got a rock, Charlie Brown! /
):   31901067326688
Due: **Saturday, March 9, 2024**
Messages:
Item checked out.

Total items: 6
Account balance: $0.00
Ready for pickup: 0
1/17/2024 11:53 AM

Renew on line or by phone
ccclib.org
1-800-984-4636

Have a great day

The sun is shining.

Aaron is hot.

Aaron is thirsty.

Splash!

Aaron gets wet.

Now he is cool.

Aaron is hungry.

He is thinking
about food.

Aaron finds

a fruit tree.

Aaron picks some.

The fruit looks
good to eat.

It is a lemon tree.

Uh-oh, Aaron!

Lemons are sour.

So Aaron makes
a big, big sandwich.

He is going to bite
his big, big sandwich.

Aaron ate

his big, big sandwich.

Maybe he ate
too much.
Poor Aaron!

Aaron loves music.

He plays

the harmonica.

He plays the cello.

Aaron plays
the trumpet.

His friend plays
the violin.

Aaron can play
the drum, too!

Aaron likes to fish.

Aaron thinks
he has caught
a big fish.

But Aaron did not

catch a fish!

Aaron caught Aaron!